The Orchard Book of
Aesop's
Fables

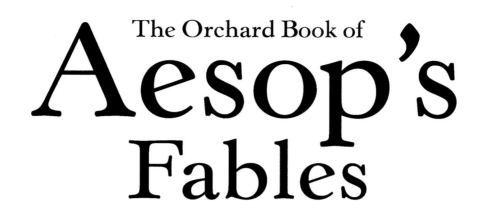

To Molly, her book and her mum's too. – M.M.

For Rupert – E.C.C.

ORCHARD BOOKS

First published in Great Britain in 2004 by Orchard Books
New edition published in 2014, 2017 by The Watts Publishing Group

19 20 18

Text © Michael Morpurgo, 2004
Illustrations © Emma Chichester Clark, 2004

A CIP catalogue record for this book is available from the British Library.

ISBN 978 1 84362 271 0

Printed and bound in Malaysia

Orchard Books
An imprint of
Hachette Children's Group
Part of The Watts Publishing Group Limited
Carmelite House
50 Victoria Embankment
London EC4Y 0DZ

An Hachette UK Company
www.hachette.co.uk

www.hachettechildrens.co.uk

The Orchard Book of
Aesop's
Fables

MICHAEL MORPURGO &
EMMA CHICHESTER CLARK

ORCHARD

CONTENTS

FOR MR AESOP FROM MR MORPURGO, A THANK YOU   6

THE LION AND THE MOUSE   8

THE HARE AND THE TORTOISE   13

THE DOG AND HIS BONE   18

THE CROW AND THE JUG   23

BELLING THE CAT   26

THE COCKEREL AND THE FOX   30

THE TRAVELLERS AND THE BEAR   34

THE WIND AND THE SUN   40

THE LION AND THE FOX   42

THE GOOSE THAT LAID THE GOLDEN EGG   46

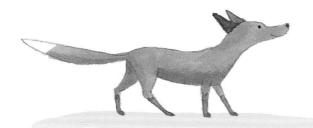

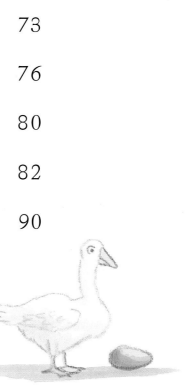

The Rat and the Elephant   49

The Heron and the Fish   54

The Dog in the Manger   56

The Miller, his Son and The Donkey   59

The Oak Tree and the River Reeds   66

The Fox and the Crow   68

The Wolf and the Donkey   73

The Sheep and the Pig   76

The Peacock and the Crane   80

The Town Mouse and the Country Mouse   82

The Wolf and the Shepherd's Son   90

FOR MR AESOP FROM MR MORPURGO, A THANK YOU

THERE WAS ONCE A LION who never hunted anymore because he was too old and too tired; who didn't roar anymore because he was too sad. So he spent all day and every day in his cave feeling very bored and very hungry. All the animals who passed by would stop and tease him. "Who's roaring now?" they'd chant.

One morning he woke up and saw a young man sitting reading a book at the mouth of his cave.

"What are you reading?" asked Lion.

"Some stories," replied the young man. "I've just written a story about you; about an old lion who won't leave his cave because he feels he's too old. He feels he's not what he was, a bit slow, a bit stupid."

"What happens to him?" asked Lion.

"He meets a young man one day called Aesop, a storyteller, who comes to his cave and reads him all the fables he has written.

And the lion loves the stories so much he wants to read them again himself."

"What happens next?" asked Lion.

"That's up to you," said Aesop. And leaving him the book, he went on his way.

Sitting at the mouth of his cave the next morning Lion roared and roared so loud that all the animals heard and came running to the cave at once.

"My friends," said Lion, "come into my cave and I will read you the best stories ever written." And they did. All the animals marvelled at Lion and how clever he was.

"This lion may be old and slow," they thought, "but this lion is not stupid."

Story after story he read, and after each one explained the moral of the story. All afternoon, all evening, all night, he read, so that one by one the animals dropped off to sleep. By morning he'd finished all of Aesop's fables and he'd also eaten up all his sleeping listeners too.

A STORY IS AS GOOD AS A FEAST.
BUT WATCH OUT YOU DON'T GO TO SLEEP!

THE LION
AND THE MOUSE

ONE HOT AFTERNOON, Lion lay snoozing happily in the shade of a tree. Suddenly he felt something running over his nose. He opened one eye and saw it was a tiny mouse. Furious at being woken, he waited his moment then he flashed out his great paw and caught Mouse by his tail.

"Oh please," squeaked Mouse, "I didn't mean to wake you. Let me go, please. I'll pay you back one day, I promise."

Lion roared with laughter, "You repay me? A little tiddley thing like you! How could such a puny creature be any use to a King of the Beasts like me?"

"Please great King," cried Mouse, "don't eat me."

Lion yawned and thought about it. He was too sleepy.

"Oh well. If you insist. After all, you wouldn't make much of a meal, would you? Off you go and be careful whose nose you walk on in future."

It was not long after that Mouse and Lion met again. This is how it happened. Lion had gone off hunting at dusk. He was stalking through the trees, following a herd of zebra, when he happened to spring a hunter's trap. A great net came down on him and held him fast. He roared and raged but in spite of all his great strength, he could not break free. His roaring echoed through the forest so that everyone heard him and everyone knew that Lion was in trouble.

Mouse heard him too, and he was a mouse of his word. Off he went as fast as his little legs would carry him to see if he could help. It wasn't long before he came across Lion still caught up in the net, still roaring and raging. "Don't worry," said Mouse. "I'll soon have you out of that." And he began to gnaw at the net ropes one by one, until at last Lion could break free.

"There you are," said Mouse. "I told you I'd pay you back didn't I?"

"A little tiddley thing like you helping out a King of the Beasts like me," Lion replied. "Who'd have thought it possible?"

"Everything is possible," said Mouse. "Goodbye Lion." And off he scampered, away into the long grass.

KINDNESS IS MORE IMPORTANT
THAN STRENGTH.

THE HARE AND THE TORTOISE

ONE DAY IN MARCH, after a morning of carefree cavorting and capering with her friends on the hillside, Hare was haring her way home along a track when she came across Tortoise. Tortoise was going the same way but slowly, very slowly, as tortoises do. Hare stopped to tease him, "Can't you go a little faster? I mean, how do you ever arrive?"

"Oh I arrive," said Tortoise very politely. "I always arrive and sooner rather than later. Maybe sooner than you imagine."

"True," said Fox who was passing by. "I'm telling you, as tortoises go, this is a very speedy tortoise."

"Speedy tortoise!" scoffed Hare. "No such thing."

"Listen, Hare," said Tortoise losing his patience a little, "I get where I want fast enough, thank you. I'll prove it if you like. How about a race? You and me. The first one to the river is the winner."

Hare leapt with laughter (keeping her distance from Fox of course). "A race! You and me? No problem. I'll beat you easy peasy. You won't see me for dust. You set us off Fox. I'm ready." And Fox agreed.

"Ready, steady, go!" Fox called out. And off they went, Hare as fast as the wind, and Tortoise...well, Tortoise as slow as a tortoise.

But Hare raced away and was very soon out of sight. So when she next looked behind her, Tortoise was nowhere to be seen. Hare thought to herself, "There's no point in showing off if no one's watching. I'll just lie down here in the sun and have a nap and wait until Tortoise comes. No worries." And before she knew it she was very fast asleep.

Meanwhile, Tortoise just kept plodding on, slowly, steadily until at last he came to where Hare lay sleeping on the grass. And he thought to himself with a smile, "Hare looks tired out with all that running, poor old thing. Best not to wake her."

On he went, slowly, steadily up the hills and down the dales towards the river.

Just then a fly landed on Hare's nose. She woke with a start and at once remembered the race. She hared over the fields as fast she could go. But it was too late. By the time she reached the river bank, Tortoise was already drinking. "What kept you, Hare?" he asked. But Hare walked off in a huff, far too cross with herself to reply. And Fox laughed himself silly all the way home.

SPEED ISN'T EVERYTHING.
THERE ARE OTHER WAYS OF WINNING.

17

THE DOG
AND HIS BONE

A DOG WAS WAITING outside the butcher's shop one day, as he often did, looking as hangdog and sad as he could. As usual the butcher soon saw him, took pity on him and threw him a bone. Off the dog trotted happy as could be, his tail wagging as he went, thinking of where he would bury the bone and how good it would taste after a week or two.

As he neared his home, he had to cross a little footbridge over a stream. He was padding across when he stopped to look down at the water because he was rather thirsty.

He was trying to work out how he could keep hold of
the bone in his mouth and have a drink at the same
time, when he noticed another dog gazing back up at
him out of the water; a bigger dog who had a very
much bigger bone in his mouth than he had.

"That's not fair," he thought, "his bone's bigger

than mine, and I want it." With that he jumped into the river and made a grab for the other dog's bone. But to do that he had to drop his own first.

Only then, as he saw his bone sinking to the bottom of the river, did he realise the mistake he had made, how silly he had been. There had been no other dog, no other bone, only his own reflection in the water.

He clambered out of the river, shook himself dry and walked off home, his tail between his legs, feeling very stupid and very cross with himself.

ENOUGH IS AS GOOD AS A FEAST.
DON'T BE GREEDY.

THE CROW AND THE JUG

IT WAS BONE DRY IN THE COUNTRYSIDE. There had been no rain for weeks on end now. For all the animals and birds it had been a terrible time. To find even a drop of water to drink was almost impossible for them.

But the crow, being the cleverest of birds, always managed to find just enough water to keep himself alive.

One morning, as he flew over a cottage, he saw a jug standing nearby. The crow knew of course that jugs were for water, and as he flew down he could smell the water inside. He landed and hopped closer to have a look.

And sure enough there was some water at the bottom. Not much maybe, but a little water was a lot better than no water at all.

The crow stuck his head into the jug to drink; but his beak, long though it was, would not reach far enough down, no matter how hard he pushed. He tried and he tried, but it was no good. However, he knew that one way or another he had to drink that water. He stood there by the jug, wondering what he was going to do. Then he saw pebbles lying on the ground nearby and that gave him a brilliant idea.

One by one he picked them up and dropped them into the jug. As each pebble fell to the bottom, so the water in the jug rose higher, then higher and higher, until the crow had dropped so many pebbles in, that the water was overflowing. Now he could drink and drink his fill. "What a clever crow," he thought as he drank. "What a clever crow."

WHERE THERE'S A WILL, THERE'S A WAY.
BUT IT HELPS IF YOU USE YOUR BRAIN.

BELLING
THE CAT

SOMETHING HAD TO BE DONE. The farm cat, with his sharp eyes and his sharp claws, had killed off so many mice that those that were left held a crisis meeting to see what, if anything, could be done to stop him.

They were all very upset, of course. "Kill him!" they cried. "Squash him!" "Pull out his claws!"

Finally the chief mouse, who was the oldest mouse too, had had enough. He called the meeting to order. "Fellow mice, let us be sensible. WE can't kill him, or squash him, or pull out his claws," he said.

"He's too strong, too big, too cunning. Wherever we go, he's always waiting to pounce – that's our problem. Now, if we knew where he was, then he couldn't creep up on us like he does and surprise us."

But try as they did, none of the mice could come up with a plan that would really work... Until one bright, young mouse had a great idea. "Why don't we..." he began, "why don't we wait till the cat's fast asleep? Then we could creep up on him and tie a bell round his neck.

That way we'll always hear him coming and we can run off before he catches us. Am I brilliant or what?"

"Yes!" they all cried. "Brilliant!"

"That mouse is a genius!"

"Let's do it! Let's do it!"

When they had all calmed down a little, the chief mouse said, "That sounds a fine plan, but there's just one little thing that worries me. Which of you will put the bell around the cat's neck?"

At this there was a long silence, while everyone looked at everyone else. "Pity," said the chief mouse. "We'll have to think again, won't we?"

SAYING SOMETHING SHOULD BE DONE
IS ONE THING. DOING IT IS
OFTEN ALTOGETHER MORE DIFFICULT.

THE COCKEREL
AND THE FOX

IT WAS A LOVELY SUMMER'S EVENING with the setting sun glowing gold in the west. For the cockerel it was time to roost. So he flew up into his roosting tree, alongside his hens, and crowed at the sunset as he always did. It was his way of saying, "Goodnight, my hens. Sleep well. Don't worry. I'm here to look after you."

He was just about to tuck his head under his wing and go to sleep, when he noticed a fox trotting through the grass below him. The fox lifted his nose and saw the cockerel and his hens. He licked his lips.

30

"Have you heard the good news, friend?" said the fox.

"What good news?" replied the cockerel, a little suspicious.

"It's peace. It's peace at last. All the animals have agreed never to chase each other or eat each other again. We can all be friends. Isn't that wonderful?"

"If you say so," said the cockerel, but he was even more suspicious now.

"It's the happiest day of my life," the fox went on. "I want to hug everyone. Come down, why don't you? Let's celebrate our new friendship."

The cockerel thought for a while. "If what you say is true," he said, "then it's the happiest day of my life too, and..." He stretched his neck and looked into the distance. "I can't be sure," he went on, "but I think I see a couple of dogs coming this way, hard on your scent. They must have heard the good news too."

In an instant the fox was off and running.

"What's up?" the cockerel crowed after him. "I thought us animals were all friends now."

"Maybe. Or maybe they haven't heard about it," replied the fox. "I'm not going to hang around to find out." And he was gone, through the hedge and away.

The hens clucked and preened themselves. "How clever you are!" they cried.

"Yes I am, my hens," said the cockerel. "Cleverer than that crafty old fox anyway." And he tucked his head under his wing and slept as the last of the sun left the sky.

DON'T BELIEVE EVERYTHING YOU HEAR,
EVEN IF YOU WANT TO BELIEVE IT.

THE TRAVELLERS
AND THE BEAR

ONE SUMMER EVENING LATE, two travellers, an older one and a younger one, were walking through a forest. All of a sudden they heard below them a great crashing and a terrible roaring.

A huge, black bear came lumbering out of the forest. One look was enough. They both ran for their lives. But the bear was running faster than they were. He was catching them up all the time.

"Hide!" cried the older traveller. "We must find somewhere to hide."

But they were out of the forest by now and there was nowhere to hide.

Suddenly the younger traveller saw his chance of escape, a single tree by the side of the road. "I'm climbing that tree," he cried.

Quick as a flash, he shimmied up the tree to safety. But there was no time for his friend to climb up after him, and the bear was coming closer and closer and closer...

Then the older one had a sudden idea. He remembered

hearing once that a bear is not interested in eating dead bodies. He would pretend to be dead! He lay down on the path and stayed quite still, not even breathing.

From the safety of his tree the younger traveller looked on in horror as the bear pawed his friend's stiff body and sniffed and snuffled at his head.

After a while the bear had had enough. He gave him one last lick on his ear and his neck and then just walked off. The younger traveller waited for a while to be sure that the bear wasn't coming back, then climbed down the tree and ran to his friend.

"Are you all right?" he cried.

"Fine," said his friend, sitting up.

"I thought you were done for, I really did," said the younger traveller.

"Me too," replied the other one.

"It was funny," said the younger traveller, helping his friend to his feet, "but when the bear was sniffing you it looked almost as if he was whispering to you."

"He was," replied the older traveller. "He told me I should pick my friends better. That anyone who saves himself first and then abandons you to your fate can't be much of a friend."

FAIRWEATHER FRIENDS
AREN'T WORTH HAVING.

THE WIND
AND THE SUN

THE WIND AND THE SUN were always squabbling.
"I can out-shine you," said Sun.

"I can out-blow you," said Wind. Then a shepherd passed by, wrapped up against the cold in a great cloak.

"All right," said Sun, "let's settle this once and for all. Whichever of us can somehow part this shepherd from his cloak is the stronger. Agreed?"

"Easy," said Wind, "watch this." He took a deep breath and blew with all his might. The shepherd felt his cloak whipping about him and just pulled it tighter.

The more Wind blew, the tighter the shepherd clung on to his cloak because he wanted to keep warm and he did not want to lose it. No matter how hard Wind blew, he could not part the shepherd from his cloak.

"My turn," said Sun, "watch this." And with that she shone down on the shepherd with all her might. Feeling the sudden warmth the shepherd loosened his cloak. As he walked on he became hotter and hotter under the burning sun. "I can't go on in this heat," he said. So he threw his cloak aside and sat down in the shade of a spreading oak tree.

"Well?" smiled Sun.

"Poof!" snorted Wind.

"Phew!" said the shepherd. "It's a glorious summer's day!"

GENTLE PERSUASION IS
OFTEN THE BEST.

THE LION
AND THE FOX

THERE ONCE LIVED A VERY OLD LION, so old that his teeth and claws were worn down and blunt with age, and so slow he could no longer chase his prey. So he worked out a cunning plan. Instead of hunting his prey, as he had before, he would invite his prey to come to him.

This is how he did it.

He told all the animals who passed by his cave that he was sick and likely to die soon, and he'd just like someone to talk to. Several of them, the most foolish, came to visit him, believing themselves to be quite safe.

42

And of course he gobbled them up.

One day a fox came along, a wily fox. He kept a
safe distance from the cave. "I heard you were sick,"
he said. "What's the matter?"

"Come a little closer," said the lion, "and I'll tell you.
I'm so weak these days I can only talk in a whisper."

But the fox was not stupid. "I think I'll stay where I am," he said. "You see, I've noticed that there are dozens of footprints going into your cave, and strangely enough there are none coming out. I wonder why that is?"

LEARN THE IMPORTANT LESSONS OF LIFE
FROM THE MISTAKES OF OTHERS.

THE GOOSE
THAT LAID THE GOLDEN EGG

THERE WAS ONCE A YOUNG FARMER who had only one dream – he wanted to get as rich as he could, as quickly as he could. One morning he went out as usual to fetch an egg from his goose for his breakfast. He reached in under her warm, soft feathers and found, as he had hoped, one huge egg. But when he looked at it he was amazed.

This was no ordinary white goose egg. It was
gold and shining in the sun, and it was so
heavy he almost dropped it. It
was solid gold. Gold! Gold!
The young farmer could not
believe his luck. His dream had come
true. Every day his wonderful goose
laid another golden egg and every day he became richer.
But the young farmer was a man in a hurry. For him,
one golden goose egg a day was not enough.
"I'm getting rich," he thought, "but
I'm not getting rich
quickly enough. All
she can lay me is one
golden egg a day.

I know what I'll do. I'll kill her," said the young farmer suddenly. "There's bound to be dozens of golden eggs inside her. That way I'll get really rich, and quickly too."

So he took his goose by the neck and killed her. And what did he discover? There wasn't a single golden egg inside her, not one. "What have I done?" he cried. "Now she is dead she won't lay me any more golden eggs. I am ruined! Ruined! Ruined!"

BE HAPPY WITH WHAT YOU'VE GOT, AND LOOK AFTER IT.

THE RAT AND THE ELEPHANT

THERE ONCE WAS A LITTLE RAT who was very proud of himself. To be honest, he did not have that much to be proud of at all, because he was a rat – and we all know what rats are like.

Anyway, one day this proud little rat was scurrying along from one farm to another looking for more grain to steal, when he saw a huge procession coming up the road. There were trumpets sounding, drums beating, cymbals clashing. The rat knew very well who this must be.

It was the king and all his retinue of courtiers. He could see the king now, riding high on a huge elephant. The elephant was adorned with glowing gold and glittering jewels. And with the king, high in his royal howdah, were the king's dog and the king's cat. Dozens of people stood at the roadside wondering at the sumptuous beauty of the king's elephant, gasping in admiration as he passed by.

As the rat came closer no one in the crowd even noticed he was there, so entranced were they by the magnificence and splendour of the king's elephant. The rat was most upset. If there was one thing he hated, it was being ignored. His pride was hurt.

"Nincompoops!" he cried. "You're a bunch of ignorant nincompoops. What is the matter with you?

Is it because the king's elephant is so big and lumpy and clumsy that you admire him so? Or is it because of his plodding feet, or his weepy eyes, or his wrinkly old hide? Look at me! I've got four legs like him, haven't I, two ears, two eyes? So I'm just as important as he is, aren't I? Look at ME!"

Just then the king's cat did look at him. And he did

not like rats, not one bit. He sprang down off the howdah and was after the rat, chasing him along the ditch until... Well, I won't tell you what happened. You'll just have to imagine it. One thing's for sure though, the proud little rat found out he was NOT quite as important as he thought he was.

THINKING YOURSELF IMPORTANT
IS NOT THE SAME THING
AS BEING IMPORTANT.

THE HERON
AND THE FISH

ONE DAY A HERON was out fishing in his favourite stretch of river. He stood there still as a statue, his long, sharp bill ready to stab a tasty fish. All about his legs the fish swarmed, not even noticing him. The heron waited and waited.

"These fish aren't big enough for me," he said. "I'll wait until a big one comes along." So he waited and waited and still there were plenty of fish, but always too small. "I don't want a snack.

I want a proper meal," thought the heron. So he waited even longer.

Suddenly all the fish left the shallows and moved away, out into the deep water in the middle of the river. Now there were no fish for the heron to catch, not even small ones.

"Drat!" he said to himself. "I shouldn't have waited so long." And all he had for his breakfast was snail – a tiny, green snail.

TAKE WHAT COMES TO YOU.
DON'T BE PICKY.

THE DOG IN THE MANGER

THERE ONCE WAS A LAZY, OLD FARM DOG who loved sleep. And his favourite place to sleep was in the cow barn, in a manger full of soft hay. One evening he was snoozing away happily in the manger when the cows came in. They'd been working all day out in the fields pulling the plough and were very tired and hungry.

"Do you mind?" they said, quite politely. "But you're lying on our hay. We're rather hungry and we'd very much like to eat it."

"I don't care how hungry you are," barked the dog. "I'm not moving." And he snarled and growled at them so fiercely that they dared come no closer.

"Look," said one of the cows, "you eat meat, don't you? This is hay. We eat hay and we're hungry."

Just then the farmer came in. "You stupid mutt, you!" he cried, and he drove the dog out of the barn, out into the cold, just to teach him a lesson.

IF IT'S NO USE TO YOU,
THEN LET SOMEONE ELSE HAVE IT.

THE MILLER, HIS SON AND THE DONKEY

ONE MORNING AN OLD MILLER and his son set out for market. With them went their donkey which they were hoping to sell that day. They went along slowly, driving the donkey instead of riding her, because the miller and his son knew they'd have a much better chance of selling her if she didn't look too tired.

But as they went on their way they met up with some friends who laughed at them as they went by. "Will you look at that? Why are you walking when one of you could perfectly well ride? How stupid can you get?"

The miller was a proud man and did not like to be laughed at.

"All right," he told his son, "you ride and I'll walk."

So his son climbed up on the donkey and off they went again.

They hadn't gone far when they came upon some travellers resting by the side of the road. "Will you look at that!" they cried. "A young man like you riding, while your poor, old father walks. Disgraceful! Have you no respect? Get down young fellow and let the old man ride."

The miller hated any arguments of any kind. "Good idea," he said. "Get down, son, and let me ride."

And so they went on their way to market.

As they neared town they passed by some women washing clothes in a stream. "Will you look at that!" they cried. "That poor boy has to walk while that old fellow has a nice, easy ride. Shame on you, old man.

You should let him ride up with you."

"If you say so," sighed the miller, not wanting to upset them. "Up you get, son. We'll ride together."

So now as they came into town they were both riding together on the donkey, who was looking rather tired and fed up by this time.

The moment the market traders saw them coming,

they ran out to protest. "Will you look at that!" they cried. "You should be ashamed of yourselves loading up a poor old donkey like that. She's tired out, poor old thing. Both of you look pretty strong and fit. Instead of just sitting there, weighing her down, you should get off and carry her."

"I hadn't thought of that," said the miller. "We'll give it a try."

They tied the donkey's feet to a pole, hoisted her up and off they went carrying the donkey between them, slung on the pole. When the townsfolk saw them they laughed and guffawed and jeered.

The donkey did not like being carried at all, and she didn't like being laughed at either. So she began to struggle and kick and bray. "Eeeyore! Eeeyore!" She kicked so hard the pole snapped and the ropes broke. Once free and back on her feet she ran off into the crowd and escaped.

No matter how hard the old miller and his son looked for her they never found her again. So in the end they went back home feeling very stupid, for they had lost their donkey as well as their dignity.

IF YOU TRY TO PLEASE EVERYONE,
YOU END UP PLEASING NO ONE.

THE OAK TREE
AND THE RIVER REEDS

THERE ONCE STOOD A GIANT OAK TREE, its great branches shading the silver river beneath it. Along the river's edge was a bank of reeds. Whenever the wind blew, they hung their heads and sang a sad song. The giant oak tree felt sorry for them.

"I am so lucky," he said. "When the wind blows, I just rustle my leaves and sing a happy tune. I know no storm could ever bend me as it bends you."

Just then the reeds began to tremble. A storm was coming in from the north. By nightfall the storm had become a raging hurricane. The great oak was not afraid. He stood strong against it. Below, the reeds were bent almost to the ground. Soon the ground was soaked with rain, and the roots of the great oak tree began to loosen. His leaves became wet and heavy. Still he did not bend. Then there was one mighty gust of wind. Up came the roots and over went the great oak tree, crashing down into the river.

When the storm had passed, the reeds were still there singing their sad song; a lament for the great oak tree, who lay like a fallen warrior, his battle lost.

OBSTINACY MAY LOOK LIKE STRENGTH.
IT RARELY IS.

THE FOX AND THE CROW

OUT HUNTING ONE MORNING, Fox lifted his nose in the air and smelt something he liked, something he liked a lot. "Cheese," he said and licked his lips. And off he went, following where his nose led him.

Suddenly he saw just what he was looking for. There was Crow sitting on the branch of an old oak tree, and in her beak a great chunk of cheese.

"Delicious," thought Fox, his mouth watering. "And just perfect for my breakfast. But how do I get it?" And then he had an idea.

"Good morning, Crow," he said. "You beautiful, gorgeous creature."

But Crow wasn't that stupid. She knew what Fox was up to. She wouldn't say a word. She would keep her cheese clamped securely in her beak. She knew the game.

Fox just sat there gazing up at her. "I have never in all my life set eyes on such a bird as you. Beside you, a peacock looks like a sparrow. You are indeed a bird of paradise. The gloss of your feathers, your delicate head, your charming eyes, your pretty little feet. Perfect in every detail. A veritable wonder of creation."

Crow was listening to this from high on her branch, and loving every word she was hearing.

"Though I wonder," Fox said. "Can any creature be that wonderful? If you could sing beautifully too, then you would indeed be the Queen of all the birds. But..." he went on, "it's too much to hope for. Not even you could be that perfect."

"Oh no?" thought Crow. "I'll show you, Fox. I'll show you how beautifully I can sing. Listen to this." And she opened her beak to sing.

Crows can't sing of course, but they can caw and they can croak. As she cawed and she croaked the cheese fell out of her beak and down, straight into Fox's waiting mouth. Fox caught it and swallowed it up at once.

Licking his lips afterwards, Fox smiled upwards at Crow who was hopping up and down on her branch in fury. "Cool it, Crow. Ugly you can't help. But how did you get to be that stupid?" And off he trotted to look for another breakfast, because for a fox two breakfasts are always better than one.

LOOK OUT FOR FLATTERERS.
THEY MAY MAKE YOU FEEL GOOD BUT
THEY'LL TAKE EVERYTHING YOU'VE GOT.

THE WOLF
AND THE DONKEY

A DONKEY WAS GRAZING AWAY HAPPILY by the edge of a wood one day, when she saw a wolf skulking through the trees like a shadow. It was too late to run away; the donkey knew that. She knew that she would have to use her wits if she wanted to save herself. So as she grazed she began to limp, hobbling along and making out that she was in the most dreadful pain.

The wolf was in no hurry and being the inquisitive type he wanted to know what the matter was. "How very kind of you to ask," replied the donkey.

"I've got this blackthorn in my hoof and I can't get it out. You wouldn't get it out would you? I'd be most obliged. I know you're going to kill me, and I really wouldn't want you to choke on it when you ate me up."

"That's thoughtful of you," said the wolf. "Tell you what. You lift up your hoof and I'll pull it out. No trouble." And the wolf came close and lay down right behind the donkey's back feet. The donkey lifted her hoof and then lashed out behind herself, sending the wolf flying.

Before he could get up again the donkey had made her escape and was nowhere to be seen.

"What a nitwit I am," said the wolf, nursing his bruises. "What was I thinking of? I'm not a doctor, I'm a hunter. And in future I'd better remember it."

STICK TO WHAT YOU KNOW,
AND BE TRUE TO YOURSELF.

THE SHEEP
AND THE PIG

ONE DAY AS THE SHEEP WERE GRAZING contentedly in their meadow, a pig wandered in and began to graze with them. The shepherd, half asleep nearby, suddenly heard a great grunting and a snuffling and a snorting. "I like a nice piece of pork," he thought. "I'll take you off to the butcher's shop. But first I've got to catch you." Quick as you like, he was on his feet and chasing after the pig. The poor pig gave him a bit of a run around, but in the end the shepherd cornered her and grabbed her. Then, tucking the pig under his arm, he set off towards the town.

The pig wasn't grunting or snorting now. She was
squealing and squeaking and struggling to escape. The
sheep followed along after them, at first just puzzled at
this noise and fuss, then quite upset by all the squealing.

"There's no need to make such a terrible din," said
one of the sheep. "He's always catching us and carrying

us off. We'd never make such a great hullabaloo. You are a cry baby."

"Cry baby?" cried the pig, still squealing, still kicking. "Hullabaloo? Listen, maybe when he catches you he doesn't hurt you. After all, when he catches you all he wants is the wool off your back. With me it's a little different if you think about it. He wants my pork, he wants my bacon. So I've plenty to squeal about, haven't I?"

BEING BRAVE WHEN THERE'S NO DANGER
IS NOT BEING BRAVE AT ALL.

THE PEACOCK
AND THE CRANE

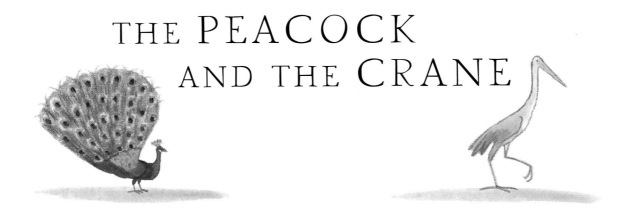

THERE ONCE WAS A PEACOCK who thought of little else but his own beauty. Whenever the sun shone he would spread his wonderful tail feathers and strut about the place simply showing himself off.

One day a crane landed nearby to hunt for frogs. The peacock strutted back and forth and screeched at the crane to look at him – but the crane was far too busy hunting frogs. The peacock became angrier and angrier.

"Hey, Crane! Take a look at me. Did you ever see anything so beautiful?"

The crane ignored him and just went on with his hunting. This made the peacock really mad.

"What's it like to be so ugly, Crane?" he cried, "To have a beak too big for your head, to be all lanky and spindly, and to have such dull, grey feathers."

At this moment the crane caught a frog, swallowed it and at once flew off, circling above the peacock. "Who cares what I look like?" he called. "At least I can fly. You can't!" And away he flew, leaving the peacock feeling very silly indeed.

JUST LOOKING GOOD
GETS YOU NOWHERE.

THE TOWN MOUSE
AND THE COUNTRY MOUSE

Town Mouse decided one day that he would visit his cousin who lived way out in the countryside. Country Mouse greeted him warmly and sat him down to a great feast of corn and hazelnuts and berries. "Help yourself," she said, "you've come a long way and must be very hungry."

Town Mouse didn't much like this plain country food. But he did not want to upset Country Mouse so he nibbled a little bit here and a little bit there and said how nice it was.

After lunch Country Mouse proudly showed Town Mouse over the fields and woods around her home. Town Mouse  thought it very dull and ordinary. But he did not say so. Instead he talked all the while about how much fun it was to live in the town, how exciting it was, and how you could eat any food you wanted. As he talked Country Mouse listened, thinking to herself how wonderful it must be to live in the town.

All night long as they slept in her snug little nest in the hedgerow, Country Mouse dreamed of life in the big town.

Next morning, Town Mouse was still bragging about how much better it was to live in the town. "You should come home with me," he said. "I'll show you things you never even dreamed of." But Country Mouse HAD dreamed of them and she wanted to find out if her dreams were true. "I'll come," she said. And off they went to town that very day.

At first it was even better than Country Mouse had dreamed. Town Mouse clearly lived in great style, exactly as he had said.

When they arrived at Town Mouse's house, lunch had just finished and there were plenty of leftovers on the table; any amount of scrumptious cheese and yummy cakes and succulent jellies. "Help yourself," said Town Mouse.

Country Mouse thought she had come to Mouse Heaven. "This is the life for me," she said.

But just as she did this, the house cat sprang up on to the table and came skittering after them. In and out of the dishes they went, the cat close behind. "Follow me," cried Town Mouse as they ran for their lives. And they only just made it too, darting down the table cloth and running helter-skelter across the carpet towards the mouse house in the skirting boards.

It was some time before even Town Mouse dared to venture out of the hole again. Still Country Mouse did not want to leave. She was terrified. "It'll be fine now," said Town Mouse. "The cat's gone. Don't worry." So Country Mouse followed Town Mouse across the carpet, hoping against hope that he was right, that the cat would not be waiting to pounce on them again.

The cat didn't come back... But the dog did. He came bounding after them, hackles up, barking his head off, sending them both scampering back to their hole for safety.

He frightened them both so much that neither dared to come out again until the following morning.

"That's it," said Country Mouse, "I'm off. You may have all the goodies a mouse could ever want in your town house, but I'm off back to the country for the quiet life."

BETTER TO BE HAPPY WITH
WHAT YOU NEED THAN RISK
EVERYTHING FOR MORE.

THE WOLF AND THE SHEPHERD'S SON

THE SHEPHERD thought his son was old enough now to guard sheep all by himself. So one morning he sent him off with the flock into the hills. "What if a wolf comes along?" the boy asked.

"Just give us a shout," his father replied, "and we'll come and frighten him off."

Day after day the shepherd's son watched over his father's sheep. The days were hot and long. Nothing ever seemed to happen and the boy became very bored and fed up. So he thought he'd make something

happen – just for fun.

Leaving his sheep he ran over the hill, waving his arms and shouting as loud as could, "Wolf! Wolf!"

Just as he had hoped, all the villagers, his father amongst them, stopped everything they were doing

and came running with their sticks to drive away the wolf.

But of course, as they soon discovered, there WAS no wolf.

"Fooled you! Fooled you!" laughed the shepherd's son. But neither his father nor the villagers thought it was funny at all.

Some days later, the shepherd's son played the same trick again.

"Wolf! Wolf!" he cried at the top of his voice, and again all the villagers came running. "Fooled you! Fooled you!" he laughed. But no one else was laughing and his father was very angry indeed.

The next day, as the shepherd's son sat watching his sheep, he really did see a wolf slinking towards the sheep through the long grass. He leapt to his feet at once and ran over the hill, shouting as loud as he could, "Wolf! Wolf!"

But neither his father nor the villagers came, because none of them believed him, not this time.